Madame Q's Dolly Mops

Dorian Shellan

Published by Haines Communications, 2024.

MADAME Q'S DOLLY MOPS

First edition. January 6, 2024.

Copyright © 2024 Dorian Shellan.

ISBN: 978-1637860359

Written by Dorian Shellan.

Table of Contents

Madame Q's Dolly Mops

by Dorian Shellan

Chapter One: Dr. Onan

Doctor Archibald Onan rang the bell at the main entrance to The Nunnery, which was promptly answered by an elegantly dressed maid. She quickly looked at his calling card as they entered the magnificent foyer. "You are expected, doctor," she said. "Please follow me."

He was led into a large sitting room where Madame Q, known to him as Anna Quinlan, rose from the couch and waved him towards an armchair. "Good afternoon, Dr. Onan," she began. "Thank you for coming. Tea?"

"Yes, please."

Anna poured two cups from the tray on the table and they both sat balancing a china saucer in their left hands while they sipped. Doctor Onan, the man who had saved her life almost a year ago, was the first person Anna contacted after returning to London from her Europe trip. She had explained her plans for The Nunnery to and he had been most accommodating in the months that followed by introducing members of The Sagamore Club to her establishment. "I am most appreciative of how you have referred gentlemen to me, and I find myself needing to ask another favor of you. You are in a unique position to assist me."

"How may I be of service, Anna?" He leaned forward to reach for a biscuit.

" I have been informed that the local constabulary is insisting on enforcing the Contagious Diseases Act, which means that unless I hire a private doctor to perform periodic examinations on my ladies they would be forced to undergo the indignation of being examined by the police doctor. I certainly cannot permit that."

"Indeed not." Dr. Onan stroked his chin. "But," he added. "Surely you must have a number of medical men in your clientele to select from?"

"Oh, I certainly do." Anna smiled broadly. "But they are all physicians."

"Ah," he responded with a knowing nod. "Performing a medical examination would most certainly be considered beneath the dignity of a London physician."

"Having an established medical practice in the city, Dr. Onan, you present with the necessary qualifications. Plus, since this position puts you in intimate knowledge of the proceedings in this house, I feel comfortable in trusting you with the requisite discretion."

"With certainty." Dr. Onan smiled. "You need have no concerns in that regard."

"It should be a straightforward process, then." Anna continued. "You'll find my ladies to be quite clean since they are thoroughly screened before I employ them, and our fee structure ensures that our clientele consists only of the most distinguished gentlemen."

Anna proceeded to offer a generous compensation package and it was agreed that Dr. Onan would return the next day to begin the examinations, which would take no more than a few days to complete. Thereafter, he would spend several days each month in her service, performing follow-up examinations and also attending to any other complaint which her ladies might have. He was to be The Nunnery's house doctor.

The ladies working at Madame Q's were remarkably different to Dr. Onan's regular patients, and he found their candor and openness to be quite refreshing. He visited each of them in their rooms at scheduled times, inquiring about their general health in addition to performing the vaginal examination for which he was hired. His easy going manner was well received, and they all gave glowing reports of his conduct and professionalism to their employer.

"You have made quite a positive impression upon my ladies, doctor," Anna told him as she poured the tea. He joined her at 4 pm every day he at The Nunnery, both for refreshment and to discuss anything that might have arisen during his consultations. "And more than one of them have inquired as to why you have not sought their favors." She smiled over her teacup. "I understand the need to remain detached and professional, doctor. But considering the nature of this business, I would like to encourage you to avail yourself of the perquisites."

"And I thank you," he responded with a smile. "But I feel more comfortable maintaining the relationships as they are."

"Really?" Anna deliberately returned her cup to its saucer and cautiously added, "Do you not like girls?"

Dr. Onan couldn't help from bursting into laughter, and he raised his right hand while composing himself. "I'm sorry," he sputtered. "Oh, yes. I very much enjoy the opposite sex. Indeed, I do. And your ladies are all lovely." He managed to contain himself again. "But I rather relish achieving the conquest almost as much as the act."

"I understand completely." Anna looked relieved as she re-filled their cups. "But how do you go about finding suitable conquests? Are they related to your practice?"

"Actually, yes. It all began when I attended to the complaint of a young wife several years ago. Her name was Evelyn. She was suffering with a painful complaint of the bladder, the symptoms of which suggested the presence of a growth.

While her concerned husband remained out of the room I asked her a series of questions, for I had the suspicion that this condition might have been accidentally self-inflicted. With a husband more than twice her age, she must surely be desirous of more than he was providing her with. 'From your symptoms, your condition could be due to one of two things,' I told her. 'The most common reason for this complaint would be a growth, which would require surgical removal.' I looked directly at her. 'But it could also be the result of a foreign object accidentally inserted during a bout of erotomania, so I have to ask you if it may be the latter."

'I confess that it is,' she admitted. 'Not wanting to commit the sin of touching myself, I attempted to find another means to purge my demons. I concluded that if I took a hair pin and made a covering for it I could then use it to deliver myself some relief without using my fingers. Unfortunately, the hairpin became dislodged and I was unable to retrieve it.'

'As embarrassing as that admission may be for you,' I told her. 'The good news is that I can easily rectify your problem without surgery. I should go and tell your worried husband right away.'

But she began to panic. 'No! He cannot know.' She grabbed my arm as I rose from my seat. 'Please tell my husband that it is a growth and I need to be operated on.' She rapidly rubbed her cheeks with the flats of her hands.

It seemed that the need to withhold this information from her husband was due to more than simple embarrassment. He would be so inflamed that he would undoubtedly have her incarcerated in a facility in an attempt to cure her erotomania. It was then that this turn of events could play directly into my hands, and a devious idea formed in my head. All I needed to do was have Evelyn feel that she was instigator, so I continued to play on her desperation by telling her that I would tell her husband that she had a cyst, which I would remove in my surgery the next day.

So, the next day, I discovered that the hair pin, instead of getting into the entrance she had intended, had slipped into the urethra. I was able to remove it with only slight discomfort to her, after which I suggested she lie down for a while.

'I am grateful for all you have done for me doctor, and I would like to thank you. In the novels I read I know there ways other than intercourse that a woman may please a man.' She began to unbutton my trousers while I remained still, permitting her to proceed. Then, seizing my prick in her hand and drawing me to her, she commenced to kiss and toy with my member. This, as may be supposed, afforded me considerable pleasure, and I let her do what she pleased. From kissing she took to sucking, and this delicious touch of drawing lips soon inflamed me beyond all restraint. She then took my cock tightly in her grasp she made her hand pass rapidly up and down the shaft while she sucked until I became heated to the utmost and proceeded to spend in her mouth." He looked up at Anna with a grin. "She came back a few days later for a follow-up visit where, still in a state of gratitude, she proceeded to strip naked in front of me and allowed me the pleasure of her cunt, mouth, and arse. It would have been wonderful in these sessions had continued, but she and her husband moved away to the country shortly thereafter."

Anna had given him encouragement with her facial expressions as he related his adventure, and she then asked, "So, how did this adventure develop into a source of other women for you?"

"Well," he continued. "My exploits with Evelyn had provided me with tremendous insight into women. While at first I, like any other doctor, considered her sexual appetite to be deviant behavior and a prime example of erotomania. But during my times with her I began to suspect that she may not be an anomaly at all. And considering the reason, the popularity of novels amongst women, made me realize that she was perhaps more the norm. Contrary to conventional wisdom, I had learned that women were indeed sexual creatures. But oh, what frustrations women must endure. When their natural instincts ignited the flames of passion the men in their lives were likely unable to satisfy them because they were raised to believe that women did not enjoy sex and only spread their legs as a duty to their husbands. And husbands, simply seeking to get the job done for themselves, would therefore never know to arouse them. Compounding this was the societal demand that women be pure, such that the act of self-pleasure caused guilt to wrack those who sought to appease nature's incessant demands.

So, in my pondering how I might be able to satisfy the lust that my time with Evelyn had unbridled, I was then struck with a revelation. My remedy already lay within my grasp in the ever growing pool of my patients. Taking note from physicians, I had taken to inducing paroxysms in women as a means to placate the common symptoms of headache and hysteria, but surely some of them would find an interest in an altogether more pleasing remedy.

I began to purchase copies of amorous works and very soon possessed a large collection of them which I displayed prominently in a bookcase in my surgery. When a particular book would catch the eye of a patient it would lead to conversation about the contents, and I quickly learned that several of my patients were themselves collectors of exciting literature, which they were obliged to keep hidden. Their level of eagerness to talk about them enabled me to ascertain their vulnerability to my seduction. As a result, some of my patients became so appreciative of the special attention I paid to them that I was subsequently able to enjoy them in every possible way. My reading continued to introduce me to more varied diversions and I eagerly called into action anything which came with the potential to enhance my enjoyment. The pleasures I derive are proportionally as great as many of these acts themselves are indecent.

"Hmm." A thought suddenly occurred to Anna. "That being the case, doctor, I believe I may have another opportunity which should be of interest to you."

"Oh, yes?" Dr. Onan looked askance.

"Do you know what dolly mopping is?"

"No. I can't say I've ever heard that term."

"Dolly mopping is when a girl, usually a domestic like a maid, seeks to earn some extra money by occasional prostitution. It's too dangerous for her to go out on the street, so she looks to being accepted at a brothel."

"Whew! That risks losing her employment if she is found out."

"Exactly! But that need for discretion also ensures that the identity of clients and their particular quirks are also protected."

"I see."

"Now, the unfortunate aspect is that most of these girls have no idea what they're getting themselves in to, imagining dolly mopping as some sort of romantic adventure. Many don't even make it through the first time before they run back to the safety of domestic life." Anna looked squarely at her friend. "Which means I have a need for someone to break them in, so to speak. If I am to bring a dolly mop into this house she has to be willing and able to satisfy my client's needs." She grinned. "What do you say, doctor? Plundering an innocent seems more aligned to your needs. Are you interested?"

"You make a fascinating offer, Anna. Yes, that sounds delightful. But why would you even bother with dolly mops? You already provide exquisite ladies for exclusive clients."

"Because some of those exclusive gentlemen have requests which would either leave marks, or are of such a nature that ladies will not fulfill them. And, sometimes, a gentlemen may not want the company of a lady at all, but rather a pretty young thing to use as a toy."

"And obtaining that here is clearly a safer option than attempting to seduce the house staff." Dr. Onan nodded in understanding.

"One thing, though. Sometimes we are dealing with virgins, and in those cases I don't want you to take them vaginally. You can have them every other way, I want you to in fact, but there is a demand amongst the gentlemen for virgins and I them charge quite a premium for the ability to deflower one."

Chapter Two: Mary

Anna had someone specifically in mind when she was speaking to Dr. Onan. Clara, one of her ladies, in telling her about the Chester household where she was previously employed had mentioned a house maid by the name of Mary. It seemed that Mary was also in the habit of stealing peeks at Herbert Chester's private library books, although she never had the nerve to remove them as Clara had done. Clara had discovered Mary doing this, which had resulted in them sharing fantasies with each other. Mary longed for actual sexual experiences and had a taste for sweets that she could barely afford. She had confessed to Clara that she might consider dolly mopping as a means to satisfy her wishes.

Knowing that Mary took a stroll through the park on her afternoon off, Anna and Clara waited for her there so that Clara could introduce her to Madame Q.

Mary was a beautiful young woman, just eighteen years of age. The perfect candidate for a dolly mop at The Nunnery, provided she would be willing.

"I'm not looking to leave the Chester household," Mary told Madame Q after Clara had left them alone. "They are good to me and it is solid employment. That's more than most girls like me could wish for."

"That will not be a problem, Mary. You will be able to come to The Nunnery whenever you wish, and you will be guaranteed at least a pound each time you do, even if no gentleman takes a fancy to you."

"It's very tempting, Madame Q. May I thing about it?"

"Certainly, Mary." Madame Q gave her a calling card. "Come to this address if you have further questions or would like to proceed."

"My day off is Monday," Mary said, studying the card. "Can I come by then?"

"Whatever is convenient for you." Madame Q smiled. "In the meantime," she produced a coin from her purse. "Here's half a crown for you to buy yourself some sweets."

MARY WAS SHOWN INTO Madame Q's study late morning the following Monday. "I would like to proceed," she said. "What must I do?"

"You will first have an encounter with Dr. Onan, a trusted friend of mine, who will introduce you to a few activities and determine whether this will be a suitable side occupation for you. I will be also be watching. You may stop the proceedings at any time, but if you do then you will have declined the offer. Do you accept these terms?"

"I do." Mary nodded excitedly.

"Are you a virgin?"

"I am. Is that a problem?"

"Not at all. In fact, you will still remain so after your time with Dr. Onan." She smiled at the confusion on Mary's face.

"If all goes well, you will be given the opportunity to sell your virginity at a later date, at a considerable profit to you."

Mary returned to The Nunnery the following Wednesday evening. Madame Q escorted her upstairs to a room on the third floor and introduced her to Dr. Onan who was there waiting for her. Sensing Mary's trepidation, he bade her sit next to him on the couch. "Just relax for a while," he told her, pouring two glasses of sherry as Madame Q disappeared into the next room where she could watch the proceedings.

After they finished their drinks, Dr. Onan put the empty glasses on the table and slid his arm around Mary. "Tell me, what do you expect to happen here?"

"I am to do whatever you might require of me," was her adoringly innocent response to his question, apparently unconcerned about the intentions of Dr. Onan's wandering fingers.

"First, you must relax and close your eyes," hr said, outwardly containing his excitement. "And permit me to raise up your clothing."

Her innocent acquisition to his request was delightful. After raising Mary's skirt, he unfastened her undergarments with the greatest possible delicacy before examining most minutely one of the most delicious little cunts imaginable. He looked ravenously upon her beautiful pink little slit which was shaded by the softest brown hair with a delicate little pink orifice beneath it. That was where his fingers then first touched her. He slowly parted her labia lips and gently rubbed her little clitoris, then coaxed her to open her legs wide. His cock strained against its confinement while he placed his fingers inside her now open slit. The opening was small and there was no maidenhead, but that is true of many virgins whose efforts, so prompted by nature, break through the restraint in that tender spot by the self-introduction of either their fingers or inanimate objects. Mary, clearly, was no stranger to masturbation.

She trembled as Dr. Onan continued to play with her clitoris, his attentions having the effect of exciting her. "Is this where you touch yourself?" He asked.

Mary appeared to be overcome by her feelings, and burying her head into his shoulder she muttered in the affirmative.

This sense of power he had gained over her was so highly gratifying to Dr. Onan's senses that it induced such a state of erection that he was not content that it should continue to be concealed. Quickly unfastening three buttons was enough to bring his stately toy into daylight and, with the light touch of his hand to back of her head, she understood what was required of her. She slid to her knees between his legs and caressed his member, all hard and excited as it was.

While Mary had no experience with what she was to do, her reading had provided her with sufficient knowledge necessary for practical purpose. "Well, then, my fine fellow," she exclaimed. "Let us see what we can make come out of that large round head of yours." Then suiting the action to her words she commenced the most agreeable fellatio, titillating his cock until his nerves strained to the utmost pitch of excitement. Feeling the approach of rapturous ejaculation, he grabbed her head and took control of the speed and depth of his member sliding in and out between her beautiful lips. Mary thus brought him to the emitting point, and with a sigh of heavenly enjoyment he released hot gushes deep into her mouth. "Keep sucking," he instructed. "Suck and swallow."

Mary eagerly complied, and after a few moments, he withdrew his still erect cock from between her lips, stood her up, stripped her, and laid her on the bed. She lay passively on her back and he gazed at her naked body while quickly divesting himself of his own clothing.

He lay next to her on the bed and slid his hand between her slightly parted thighs. She gasped while his fingers sought out her engorged clitoris and her breathing intensified as he brought her to the edge of orgasm. But instead of delivering Mary into rapture, he slid his moistened hand beneath her and began to toy with her bottom. "Have you ever come across reference to buggering in your reading?" He asked.

A wry smile on her aroused face confirmed the affirmative.

"Then I shall next go in there," he told her as he eased his index finger between her puckered folds.

"Yes, oh, yes," she panted. "Put yourself anywhere that you like, but first deliver me that pleasure to which you have brought me to the precipice of."

"Like this?" He teased as he once again made contact with her clitoris. He diligently worked his finger until she was reduced to gasping and unable to offer resistance as he then rolled her over. Sinking upon her still panting body, Dr. Onan's trembling fingers quickly moistened his excited member well with saliva before he put it against the tender orifice between the cheeks of her lily white bottom.

She now felt the painful pressure he was causing with the large head of my prick, but she remained obediently still while he continued his attempt to gain entrance. Initially foiled by her tightness, a sudden squirt of pre-ejaculate came to his assistance and once more trying the now moistened barrier he finally gained a penetration. The head of his prick went gradually in as far as its junction with the shaft. He took a breath and then pushed past the sphincter muscle, and after easing for a moment or two then began slowly to move in and out of her bottom, which tightly clasped his cock. Slowly repeating his thrusts, he was soon completely within the body of the dear girl.

"Oh how I burn," Mary screamed out as he lay on top of her, pinning her face down onto the bed. "How deliciously warm you feel inside me. Oh, frig me in front, doctor. Don't let us waste such heavenly pleasure."

Dr. Onan slid his hand between her belly and the sheet and proceeded to comply with her request, causing Mary's bottom to throb so convulsively that he could not refrain from spending, making her actually scream with delight as the warm balsam exploded deep inside her. He continued, ejaculating several times during this long and ecstatic bottom-fuck without withdrawing, until after about half an hour he sank upon her, almost fainting with delight, his prick still panting and throbbing.

Madame Q had watched the proceedings from her concealed position in the adjoining room with absolute delight. Not only had Mary's enthusiasm shown that she was to be an ideal dolly mop for The Nunnery, but Dr. Onan's desire for novices had also been formidably demonstrated. She grinned. This predilection of his would prove most useful.

Chapter Three: Dolly Mop Mary

When interviewing gentlemen as prospective new clients, Madame Q made a point of learning about their fantasies and desires so she would be in a position to help select the best match for them. While most of them had a preference the educated ladies who resided at the nunnery, there were a select few with fetishes such as deflowering virgins and rough, forced sex that were better discretely fulfilled by dolly mops. One such client was Sir Edward Mablethorpe. It was he that Madame Q approached regarding Mary.

"While she is indeed a virgin, Sir Edward, certified as such by our house doctor, she has been an athletic girl to date and as a result is devoid of a hymen. This provides you with a double advantage. The opportunity to be a pretty young girl's first time, and yet do so without any blood."

"Will you have her dressed the way I like?"

"Certainly. She will present as a schoolgirl in a sailor suit with a short skirt." Madame Q maintained a wardrobe of the most commonly requested outfits. She knew her clientele well.

Sir Edward smiled and enthusiastically stroked his chin.

"Twenty pounds. She will perform fellatio and you will be able to enjoy deflowering her."

"And more?"

"As always, you are free to negotiate anything else directly."

MARY, HER PASSIONS having been thoroughly aroused, now proved to be most lasciviously inclined and a desire for more. It was with enthusiasm that she responded affirmatively when Madame Q told her about the gentleman who wished to take her virginity, even before Mary was told that it would earn her five pounds.

"Will he also want to do anything else with me?" Mary asked with a smirk after Madame Q explained the upcoming scene. "I kind of liked being sodomized by Dr. Onan."

"He will need your consent for anything beyond the scope of the agreement, but if that happens he will reward you with a token of his appreciation, which will be yours to keep." Madame Q grinned. "But remember, at least initially, you are to play the innocent."

"YOU'RE A VERY PRETTY girl, Mary," Sir Edward told her after Madame Q had introduced them. "It's my pleasure to make your acquaintance."

"Thank you, sir," Mary responded demurely. "I do hope you like my outfit."

"It is perfect, my dear." His eyes looked down, then slowly rose from the little bow on her anklet socks up her legs to the hem of her skirt at mid-thigh. "Come," he said, taking her hand as we walked her across the room. "Stand here so I might further look at you,"

Mary stood attentively in front of him as he settled onto the couch before reaching forward and slowly raising up Mary's skirt. "Hold this up, that's right," he told her, then untied the ribbon holding up her undergarments. They fluttered down to her ankles.

"I would have said it was impossible to find such a pretty little slit as yours, Mary," he exclaimed, reaching forward with his right index finger. "How deliciously warm it feels." He looked up at her partially closed eyes. "Sit on the divan, for I must examine this delight more thoroughly."

He eased Mary into a recumbent posture, removed the undergarments from her ankles, flipped up her little skirt, and eased her legs apart while he knelt between them. By this attitude her thighs were stretched widely apart, and her cunt was fully exposed to his view. "Push your belly a little forward," he instructed. "There, that's right, now I have it exactly." So saying, he deliberately separated the lips of Mary's slit with his tongue, and worked it into the innermost recesses. He then moved his tongue in and out, while at the same time caressing her clitoris with his lips.

"Oh, sir," Mary moaned. "You are giving me the most intense pleasure, but if you do not desist I am going to spend."

His response was to increase the motion of his tongue, to which Mary could hold out no longer. With a convulsive heaving of her whole body, she emitted in profusion.

Sir Edward raised his smiling face. "My dear Mary," he began. "I have had the pleasure to observe your perfect cunt, I've felt it, I've played with it, and I have tasted it. But now it is time to perform the act which is the most delicious of all" He rose to his feet, took her hands, and stood her in front of him. He then slid his hands around her waist, and with an upward movement to which she compliantly raised her arms, removed her blouse.

Turning her around with her back to him, he toyed with her nipples and whispered into her left ear, "I will now take you to the bed."

He had her lie back on the bed while he removed her shoes and socks, leaving her wearing only her skirt, which he lifted up and laid across her belly.

Sir Edward's enjoyment was intense. After undressing himself, he first made her lie as still as possible, in which position he was able to prepare her for the upcoming deflowering by the gentle movements of his fingers both round and between the labia lips of her little downy cunt. Then, satisfied that she was ready, he lay on top of her and plunged his engorged prick into the tightness.

Mary gasped and clung onto his back from the pain caused by the first time entrance of manhood into her tight entrance, yet the pain also delivered her into a swoon of such pleasure that she had never felt before. "Oh, sir," she pleaded. "Fuck me with furious energy. Let me feel what the ecstasies of sexual conjunction are really like."

Sir Edward continued to pound more and more until it felt as if his prick had traversed the full extent of her belly. Then nearing that intoxicating moment, he drew out his close-to-bursting member and moved to straddle her upper body. The shining, bulbous head of his cock now only inches from her lips, he took her head in his hands and forced it into her mouth. She sucked obediently and with such relish that he could not refrain from bathing her tongue with his hot juice, but instead of having her suck him dry he pulled away from her lips, eased off her, and ordered her to roll over.

"Now, by separating your bottom cheeks," he told her as he massaged her buttocks. "I am able to reveal both your delicious little cunt and also a ravishing little wrinkled orifice which nature placed so close to it. So close, in fact, that it is impossible not to believe that it ought to always have its due share of attention. Do you not agree, Mary?'

"Please do with me as you will, sir," Mary replied. "I experience nothing but delight from the attention you bestow upon me."

Needing no further encouragement, Sir Edward moved to a position in order to satisfy himself with her twitching puckered bottom. He entered it easily, and by the third thrust his stomach was smacking into her buttocks. He laid fully across her back and whispered into her ear, "This is in fairness," as he reached beneath her in order to rub her clitoris, bringing her to climax in conjunction with his ejaculating one last time.

"WHAT DID YOU THINK of Sir Edward, Mary?" Madame Q asked at the end of the evening.

"I liked him. He took the time to warm me up and he gave me a sovereign for letting him fuck my arse." Mary giggled. "What sticks with me though is that he got a bit rougher as the session went on." She looked directly at Madame Q. "Is he one of your clients who do like it rough?"

"You're one step ahead of me, Mary. Yes, he is. And now that he's deflowered and buggered you he wants to do more with you. Are you familiar with the works of the Marquis De Sade?"

"I've heard of them, but that's all."

"Here. Read this book and let me know what you think. Sir Edward has told me that he would like to tie you up, spank you, birch you, and force you to please him. You would be paid well, but there would be lingering marks afterward such that you would need a couple of weeks away from The Nunnery if you agree."

Mary agreed enthusiastically on returning the book only days later.

AT THE APPOINTED TIME, Mary was delivered to the dungeon room, where Sir Edward was waiting, wearing were only a dressing-gown and trousers and brandishing a riding crop in his right hand. "Now, Mary," he said as he sat in a leather armchair. "You will do as I tell you and remain silent unless I direct you to speak. Do you understand?"

"Yes, sir."

"Very good. I require you to remove all of your clothing while I watch."

Mary stripped for him with excited enthusiasm and then at once became docile, standing attentively and completely naked in front of him while he moved the crop across and around her body. "Legs apart," he said, and proceeded to lightly tap her pussy with the business end.

Obeying Sir Edward's instruction, Mary then quietly placed herself on her belly upon the cushioned spanking horse in the center of the room. She remained still while he used cords to secure her by her wrists and ankles. He then finished the bondage by firmly fastening her body down by means of a silk sash passed under the horse and over her back. "Now, my dear, you are completely at my mercy!" He exclaimed while massaging her wonderfully smooth buttocks with both hands. He then eased back slightly and brought the flat of his right hand down squarely on her upturned right buttock cheek. It made a delightful sound on contact.

After a few more slap, he then increased both the frequency and severity until Mary's bottom had become bright pink. She was breathing hard and straining against the tight restraints, and Sir Edward's member had become attentive in anticipation. He moved his hand between her thighs and his fingers slid effortlessly into her vagina, eliciting such a gasp as to indicate that she was close to spending. He continued using his fingers in this way until she was almost beside herself.

"Is there something you want, Mary?"

"Oh, I must have the real thing at once," she begged. "Please stop tantalizing me so."

"Ah, but tantalizing a part of the pleasure of what the Marquis wrote." He replied, while his well lubricated fingers moved to tease her clitoris until she was driven almost mad by it. With deft manual dexterity, he keep her on the edge of orgasm until her appeals for satisfaction became absolutely desperate, then with a single thrust he completely buried his cock into her wanting cunt. She spent immediately, and before she had the opportunity to catch her breath he pulled out, moved to the other end of the bench, and forced his glistening prick into her mouth. She compliantly sucked and was rewarded almost instantly with a most plentiful shower of semen in her mouth. "That's a good girl," he told her. "Swallow it all."

After withdrawing from Mary's mouth, Sir Edward went to a cupboard and procured a fresh birch rod. "From your reading, you know that flagellation increases amorous pleasures," he said. "So I am now going to birch your bottom."

Standing at her left side, he first brushed the birch gently across her pink bottom before starting to lay into her. Her skin turned to a rosy hue as she attempted in vain to twist and wriggle as the flogging continued. When he stopped, Mary's bottom was covered with red streaks with two or three of them starting to bleed, but Mary was panting and completely given to the pleasure of the pain he had provided. Sir Edward reached between her legs and she screamed into orgasm the moment his fingers made contact with her engorged clitoris.

He then untied her, and without giving her time to compose herself eased her off the horse and placed her on her hands and knees onto the soft rug. Then, reaching for a side table, he produced a dildo, which he placed in her right hand. "You will make yourself cum again with this," he said, and then ordered her to shove it into herself.

She brought the dildo to bear against her coral sheath, it entered the lips, and in another moment it was plunged to the very hilt into her vagina. Sir Edward then placed himself behind her as she pushed the dildo in and out, and with two fingers he teased her puckered rear entrance.

A convulsive shudder ran through Mary's frame and the motion of her hand suddenly stopped, leaving the dildo still embedded in her cunt. Captivated by her delirium, Sir Edward could not restrain himself any longer and he immediately treated Mary to receive the entire length of his member up her arse. Only a few thrusts later, he too succumbed to the blissful moment of emission.

Chapter Four: Gertie

"You must tell me, doctor." Anna Quinlan leaned back slightly as she sipped her tea.

"Tell you?" Dr. Onan responded teasingly.

"Yes. Tell me about the woman you currently have in your sights."

Anna had such a way about her that, for some reason, Dr. Onan always found himself completely comfortable about opening up to her. "Well," he twisted his mouth. "Last week I was requested to call upon a retired military man recently returned from India, who was staying at a boarding house with his wife while they awaited the remodeling of their recently purchased townhouse. While her symptoms had been unsettling to them, the complaint turned out not to be particularly serious, most likely the result of the change in environment. It does require me to return every few days to check on her for the next couple of weeks, however. Anyhow, after attending to the patient, I was speaking to the owner of the house about dietary restrictions when a perky beauty, perhaps aged twenty, suddenly appeared, wiping her hands dry on a cloth. She was as upright as a dart, had a fine full face, with plenty of color in it, and a shapely form. 'Gertie,' her mother said. 'Say hello to Doctor Onan. He called here to see to the general's wife.'

'Hello, sir,' said the young lady, smiling and bobbing into a brief curtsy.

'I'm pleased to make your acquaintance, Gertie,' I responded, returning her smile.

'Run along now, Gertie,' the landlady ushed her daughter back into the kitchen and turned again to me. 'Gertie this year returned home from boarding school and she and I run the house together,' she explained. 'She's my youngest daughter, almost twenty one now. Her two older sisters are married and moved away. I scrimped to get her educated so she might also find a nice gentleman to marry.'

'She certainly is an attractive girl.' I commented as I watched Gertie disappear back into the kitchen.

'She's a fine, strapping wench, sir. Just the kind of girl I was at her age, though I think if anything she's a trifle more plump than I was.'

Listening to her mother, it was likely that Gertie was still a virgin; an innocence that makes her particularly attractive to me."

"So, how do you plan going about this conquest?"

"Business as the boarding house is slow right now since the general and his wife are her only lodgers, so its easy for me to see Gertie on my follow up visits. Her mother always offers a cup of tea and a chat whenever I stop by, and eager to pick up any tidbit of information about Gertie, I graciously accept her invitations.

Yesterday, she was fretting about her daughter. 'I don't know what I shall do with her.' She started. 'I shall have to send her into service; this place won't keep two of us. And not only that, doctor. I've been thinking that it might not hardly be the thing for a giddy girl like her to be brought into contact with gentlemen who might be staying here.'

Listening to her, I realized that she was completely unaware of my intentions towards her daughter, so merely remarked that I was surprised that such thoughts might run in her head. She did make a point to tell me how Gertie was fond of fashion, though, so I bought a small parcel of ribbons from a millinery and had them addressed to her, without saying a word as to my having sent them."

Anna simply responded with a knowing smile and offered Dr. Onan another cake.

After Dr. Onan called on his patient at the boarding house the next week he ran into Gertie as he was leaving. She was all decked out with the ribbons he had sent adorning her hat. "Good afternoon, Gertie," he said. "Where are you off to with such a pretty hat?"

"Only for a walk from this silly old inn," she replied happily. "I have a beau, doctor. An unknown beau, who has sent me all these beautiful ribbons. So I thought by going out he might see that I had appreciated his gift. That is, if he were watching for me," she added, with an ear to ear smile.

"That's a splendid idea, my girl," he told her. "Perhaps after he sees you he will send you something else."

"Oh, I do hope so," she began. "You see these splendid ribbons tends to make my hat look a little shabby."

"Then you shall have to obtain a new hat."

"Alas, doctor, I know it. But mother doesn't have a lot of money at this time, so I can't afford to buy another one." She smiled again. "At least, not just yet."

"If you'd promise not to tell your mother. And I mean, promise me sacredly, not on any account, to tell her. I will take you to a shop where I saw a lovely one yesterday that would suit your style admirably, and I will purchase it for you."

"Oh, doctor. That is so kind of you, but I could not impose."

"Oh, don't speak like that, Gertie. It would be my pleasure." He took her fingertips in his. "Now, go out into the street as if for your regular walk and wait around the corner for me. I will join you in five minutes." Of course, Dr. Onan suggested this to avoid observation by Gertie's mother.

After waiting for a few minutes he left, caught up with Gertie, and walked with her to the milliner from whom he had previously purchased the ribbons. "Good-morning, doctor," the milliner greeted them as they entered the shop. "I'm pleased to tell you that I now have that particular shade of ribbon you wanted."

The cat now being out of the bag, Gertie glanced quickly up at him. "So you are my unknown beau," she whispered. "Doctor, I am so surprised."

"And, I hope, pleased too, Gertie?"

"Well, I hardly know," she said, all a flutter. Then, suddenly distracted, added, "but, oh my, doctor. What a beautiful hat."

"Indeed it is," Dr. Onan concurred.

The milliner reached for a hat. "And this is one that will be perfect for the young lady."

Gertie gently took the hat and put it on, then turned to model it.

"Perhaps the good doctor might also like to see you in a new dress, my dear?" The shopkeeper asked.

"But, of course," Dr. Onan replied as both of them looked up to him."

THE MILLINER RIGGED Gertie up from top to toe, and before they left the shop Dr. Onan had spent over ten pounds on her. "How on earth am I to account for having this to Mother?" Gertie asked, her hands caressing her new clothes.

"We'll have them sent anonymously, just like the ribbons." Dr. Onan replied. "That way your mother can't form a guess as to where they came from. The milliner will put no address inside."

"How can I thank you for these wonderful presents," Gertie gushed as they left the store.

"My dear Gertie," Dr. Onan replied. "There is a way of showing your gratitude to me, but that way you are as yet I fear too young to understand."

"Then," she responded coyly. "Perhaps you will instruct me?" She smiled. " Isn't your surgery close by?"

Dr. Onan's cock began to strain against the confinement of his trousers. He reached his right hand out to her. "Come, my dear." He smiled. "I will take you there."

Once Dr. Onan and Gertie were alone in his surgery she stepped forward and seemed far less timorous in her manner than he had expected. "My dear Gertie," he said, placing his arm around her waist and easing her down next to him on the divan. "You are heartily welcome to what my poor purse can afford. As for those pretty matters I purchased today, kisses from those pouting lips will repay me a thousand fold." He pulled her towards himself and kissed her.

Rather than trying to disengage herself, Gertie made it clear that his caresses were not at all unwelcome.

Emboldened by her ease, Dr. Onan began unfastening the buttons of her frock, and after giving him a wry smile she allowed herself to be revealed. As her breasts were uncovered and brought into his view, he became ecstatic.. Her beautiful little nipples adorning her lily-white breasts looked like a pair of twin cherries. He leaned forward for his mouth to fasten onto one, and sucked it avidly. "Oh, Doctor Onan," she gasped as her fingers ran through his hair. "I shall surely faint if you continue to make me feel so."

"My darling," he said, taking her right hand and kissing it before directing it on top of the bulge in the front of his pants. "Did you ever feel anything like this?"

Her thumb and fingers clutched it with a firm clasp and she began to tentatively rub my cock through the fabric. Then, before, he could prevent her, she slid from his grasp into a kneeling position on the floor between his extended legs.

"Is this where you would like me, doctor," she asked timidly. "I do read novels, you know."

"What do you suggest, then, Gertie dear?" he asked.

She gave no answer, but reached out with both hands and quickly unfastened his buttons. His cock was glistening and erect and she smiled up at him sweetly while she grasped it, pulling back the foreskin to reveal my excited purple bulb. The hand which held his penis was brought softly forward, her mouth opened, and she tongued him with a sweet suck that almost drove him frantic.

For at least two minutes he lay back on the divan, his brain in a delirium of delight, until, unable to bear it any longer, he spent with such force that excess sperm spurted from the sides of her mouth and dribbled down his shaft. Continuing to suck and swallow, however, Gertie used her tongue to consume every last drop. She then slid his prick out of her mouth and looked up. "Did I do it right," she asked innocently.

"Oh, most certainly, yes."

Gertie stood up and pulled her clothing together. "I'd better get back now or mother will wonder where I am," she said, giving Dr. Onan a quick peck on the cheek. He responded with a hug, bade her good afternoon, and she happily made her way back home.

Dr. Onan stopped by the boarding house to check on his patient a few days later, and when he was finished Gertie showed up, fully decked in her new finery. "These things have come, doctor," she told him. "Mother went on like anything, but I vowed I didn't know who had sent 'em, so she told me in that case I'd better thank God, and say no more about it."

"Then it's all right, isn't it?" Dr. Onan told her, looking intently at her bust, which, confined as it was by the tightly fitting dress, showed itself to singular advantage.

"I'm afraid, doctor," she said, hands behind her back and rocking to and fro. "That I might not have thanked you sufficiently the other day, and so I thought as mother has gone out to visit her brother," she smiled. "You'd let me do it now? You can come up to my room where we'll be all alone, if you'd like."

Dr. Onan responded both affirmatively and enthusiastically, and followed her upstairs. After they entered, she closed the door softly behind her and the sat together on the couch. Dr. Onan's hand met no resistance as he slid it up under her dress. "Would you like me to strip for you, doctor?" She asked as she stood up and raised the front of her dress so he might appreciate her willingly twitching lips peeking through the down between her thighs.

Dr. Onan's expression must have signified his positive answer, for as his eyes fell onto the delicate curls adorning her mound of Venus her clothing was tossed aside. He looked up at her naked body and with maddened haste leaped to his feet to grab her and push her down on the couch. He stripped his clothes off as fast as he could, throwing them onto the floor, then lay on top of her. She had no lack of reciprocity, and as his cock discovered as it slid between her eagerly spread legs, she was by no means wanting in lubricity.

The next day, Anna asked Dr. Onan if he had been satisfied with Gertie's gratitude, then smiled knowingly as he relayed to her what had occurred. "It was not what you had expected, was it?" she asked.

"Oh, it was splendid fuck all right."

"And yet you were disappointed that she had no maidenhead."

"I had been completely taken in by her act of innocence. Not only was she not a virgin, but to me she possessed the expertise that one might seek at your premises."

"And you now realize, doctor, that your thinking regarding her innocence was simply an illusion."

Dr. Onan looked slowly nodded and sported a sideways smile. "As you always suspected?"

"Indeed! She played the role beautifully and you fell for it. No harm done, eh?"

"I suppose not," he chuckled.

"So, what do you plan to do with Gertie now," Anna inquired.

"Nothing." His response was matter-of-fact. "She has no appeal for me now."

"From what you have told me about her enthusiasm for sport, she may be well qualified to join The Nunnery as a dolly mop. Would you care to give her Madame Q's card?"

DOCTOR ONAN HAD ONE last follow up visit to his patient at the boarding house the next week, and before he left Gertie came up to him. "Would you like to come again to my room, doctor?" She asked. "I can continue to express my appreciation to you, if you like." She smirked. "And while I do like my fine hat and dress, doctor, we could make it so much easier for you to express any future generosity in monetary terms."

"I think not." Dr. Onan chuckled and slowly shook his head. "You know, your mother imagines you a virgin, Gertie."

"Oh, mother likes to play up the illusion because it helps makes a boarder notice me." She replied without any concern. "All innocent that I seem."

"So, she is in on the act?"

"Of course. We like supplement the inn's income from some of the men who stay here. You were quite a bonus."

"It is an effective ruse, Gertie. I must confess that I was well taken in."

"Well, you surely can't fault me for capitalizing on the generosity of men, can you?"

"Not at all Gertie. I quite understand. In fact, I come with a proposition for you." He produced Madame Q's calling card from his pocket.

Chapter Five: Dolly Mop Gertie

Within a few minutes after having met Madame Q, Gertie became rather emboldened and inquired how much money a girl who worked at The Nunnery could earn. Her eyes grew greedily large at Madame Q's response. "That's more than I could ever imagine," she said.

"You must know, however," Madame Q told her. "That I am very particular about the dolly mops I employ." She smiled. "First, my girls must remain free from disease. That is determined after examination by Doctor Onan."

"I like that," Gertie looked up and smirked.

"Second, dolly mops exist to cater to a myriad of deprivations, so they have to consent to doing anything that might be required of them."

"Anything?"

"And everything. Yes. Sometimes gentle, sometimes rough. I only paid them so handsomely because they relinquish their bodies to the passions and pleasures of others."

Gertie swallowed hard and looked down at the floor, but then immediately perked back up. "I understand," she said.

"If this remains of interest to you, I will offer you the opportunity to interview for the position, for which I will pay you two pounds, regardless of the outcome."

"An interview?"

"To determine your suitability, yes."

"What constitutes an interview?"

"I will watch you with a man, and require you to do anything else my fancies might devise. And do them convincingly." Madame Q rose to her feet. "If you wish to consent to being interviewed, return here at seven o'clock this evening."

DR. ONAN ARRIVED AT The Nunnery that evening. He had enthusiastically agreed to jointly interview Gertie, and was looking forward to watching Madame Q in action.

He right away went to the dungeon room where Anna, as Madame Q, was awaiting his arrival. She was completely enveloped in a silk dressing gown, her feet were encased in Persian slippers, and her legs were evidently bare. A soft warm air pervaded the room, and a fragrant and exciting perfume shed its influence around. In the center of the room was a peculiar article of furniture, which bore the appearance of a St. Andrew's Cross, placed horizontally and supported by a massive pedestal, which at one end was cut away so as to correspond with the form of the cross at its lower extremity.

"You do understand what I am proposing that we do, doctor?" She asked.

"I not only understand," He smiled at her, "But I am also most encouraged by our shared desires."

"Splendid!" She rose and rang the bell. In a few moments the door opened, and Gertie entered wearing a dress which held her bosom tightly like a corset and having short skirt which fully exposed her legs in front. She was clearly surprised at the sight of Dr. Onan also being present.

"Sit down, Gertie," said Madame Q as she locked the door, then turned to the prospective dolly mop. "Gertie," she continued. "Doctor Onan is going to fuck you while I watch to determine how well you perform. After which, I also intend to enjoy you."

"Oh! Madame," Gertie cried out with the realization of what she had just been told. "Pray, do not make me do that."

"Did you not agree to do whatever was required of you when I agreed to granting you this interview?"

"Yes, Madame," Gertie stammered. "But, but I never thought I would have to be," she swallowed. "Be with a woman."

"Ah, but you shall soon know that pleasure." Madame Q tenderly brushed a lock of hair behind Gertie's ear. I require it of all of my girls, since so often a gentleman will wish for two at the same time." She gave Gertie a matter-of-fact look. "So, now then. Are we to proceed, or shall I turn you out?"

"Please. I will do anything you want, Madame."

"Excellent! You may struggle and scream if you wish, for you are also going to be bound and birched. Your screams cannot be heard beyond this room."

Gertie swallowed hard and looked nervously towards Dr. Onan. He simply smiled back at her, very much enjoying these proceedings.

"Do you wish to proceed with your interview?" Madame asked for confirmation.

"Yes. Yes, I do, Madame."

"Very good." Madame nodded towards Dr. Onan. "Seize her."

Dr. Onan was so inflamed by feelings of ungovernable lust by this time that he was also inclined to do whatever Madame wanted. He sprang up and held Gertie fast.

"First, she must be stripped."

Gertie did not struggle as Dr. Onan slid the dress from her shoulders, then Madame Q approached and seized her arms. She held them firmly and directed the doctor to divest Gertie of her drawers, stockings, and shoes, until at last she had been rendered into a perfectly nude condition.

"We will now lift her on the cross table," Madame Q instructed.

They extended Gertie onto her back, with her legs and arms stretched out on the four branches of the cross, then securely fixed her in that position by concealed straps. There Gertie now lay, her lovely naked form bound for upcoming pleasures while her every muscle convulsed and twitched in a combination of anticipation and trepidation.

Madame Q proceeded to suck Gertie's breasts and rub her belly and the inside of her thighs, while directing Dr. Onan to fondle her cunt. He obeyed delightedly, and then proceeded to rub her clitoris with his index finger, causing her to struggle as she became more and more excited. A few moments later, she gave down a most copious spend. This was the signal Madame was waiting for. "Now, Gertie," she exclaimed, "I will watch you being properly fucked."

Dr. Onan quickly stripped to the buff, and following Madame's instructions, he approached the lower end of the cross table. He positioned himself between Gertie's legs and placed the point of his prick just within the lips of her spending cunt. Obeying Madame's command, he proceeded with a brutal lunge, and excited to madness by the helpless struggles of the poor girl, was buried in her in a moment. His ruthless prick pounded in and out while her juices trickled over his testicles and down the crack of her bottom.

Leaning forward, Madame Q then began sucking and biting the tender nipples of the victim while Dr. Onan continued to fuck Gertie with deep and full insertions of his prick, his pubic hairs slapping into hers. For a moment Gertie appeared to faint from excess of emotion, but seeing this Madame bit her bosom, and Gertie recovered consciousness with a shriek of anguish. Madame then threw off her only garment and straddled Gertie's face. "Lick me," she ordered. "Your future here depends upon how well you service me with your tongue."

Gertie's chin and head moved back and forth as she furiously worked her tongue, eliciting the most delightful moans of delight from Madame. "Good girl, that's right, oh yes," Madame shrieked as she entered into orgasmic throes with a prolific emission over Gertie's face as Dr. Onan spent within her body.

Both tormentors recovered quickly, but they were by no means finished. Reversing Gertie so that she now lay on her belly, Madame then produced a dildo, which she immediately entered into Gertie's ready cunt to the very hilt. She then proceeded with birch rods to lash her bottom, loins, inside her thighs, and even the lips of her cunt, tightly distended around the dildo, till the hue of her skin was a burning scarlet. Then, satisfied with the effect she had wrought, Madame Q removed the dildo, and pulling wide apart the cheeks of Gertie's smarting bottom, thrust it into the convulsed bottom-hole. "Now, doctor," Madame exclaimed. "You must fuck her again."

Her instructions were immediately carried into effect. His prick entered Gertie's cunt with the greatest ease, while Madame Q worked the dildo in and out of the girl's bottom. Their movements continued fast and furious until Gertie's moans became higher pitched and her breathing became faster. "She's coming," Madame announced. "She's spending."

Madame then withdrew the dildo from Gertie's bottom-hole of the now limpid girl and instructed Dr. Onan to substitute his prick. He commenced to fuck her arse, while Madame reclined on the adjacent couch, watching the spectacle with immense enjoyment. Dr. Onan soon ejaculated.

After a few moments they untied Gertie, who was soaked and utterly exhausted, and escorted her to the couch, where the three drank burgundy together. Madame caressed Gertie and told her what a good girl she had been. She then explained that the interview would be satisfactorily completed upon her kneeling between Madame Q's spread legs and pleasuring her.

The eagerness with which Gertie took to this task prompted an immediate erection from Dr. Onan, and on seeing this Madame ordered him to again sodomize the kneeling girl from behind. Each thrust he gave simultaneously pushed Gertie's tongue inside Madame's receptive cunt, quickly inducing her to spend as he felt the last of his semen pulse away.

Gertie was hired right away, and soon became established as one of Madame Q's most popular dolly mops.

THE END

About the Author

With keen interest in nineteenth and early twentieth century history, Dorian Shellan writes a variety of stories with Victorian settings.

The Victorian era was one of great innovations, industrial, medical, and social. Dorian's stories incorporate many of these changes and the impact it had on the population of that time.

Dorian's genres range from novels, including adventure and romance, to short stories, to Victorian erotica.

Read more at https://victorianstories.com.

www.ingramcontent.com/pod-product-compliance
Lightning Source LLC
Chambersburg PA
CBHW052144220626
47052CB00005B/1189